anythi

D0398443

DK READERS

BEGINNING TO READ ALONE

2

LEGO friends

Perfect Pets

Written by Lisa Stock

DK

LONDON, NEW YORK, MUNICH,
MELBOURNE, and DELHI

DK LONDON
Editor Lisa Stock
Pre-Production Producer Siu Yin Chan
Producer Louise Daly
Managing Editor Elizabeth Dowsett
Design Manager Ron Stobbart
Publishing Manager Julie Ferris
Publishing Director Simon Beecroft

DK DELHI
Assistant Editor Gaurav Joshi
Assistant Art Editor Pranika Jain
Art Editor Divya Jain
Deputy Managing Editor Chitra Subramanyam
Deputy Managing Art Editor Neha Ahuja
DTP Designer Umesh Singh Rawat
Senior DTP Designer Jagtar Singh
Pre-Production Manager Sunil Sharma

Reading Consultant
Linda B. Gambrell, Ph.D.

First American Edition, 2014
15 10 9 8 7 6 5 4 3 2
Published in the United States by DK Publishing
345 Hudson Street, New York, New York 10014

002–256566–May/14

DK books are available at special discounts when purchased in bulk for sales promotions,
premiums, fund-raising, or educational use.
For details, contact:
DK Publishing Special Markets
345 Hudson Street, New York, New York 10014
SpecialSales@dk.com

A catalog record for this book is available
from the Library of Congress.

ISBN: 978-1-4654-1984-2 (Paperback)
ISBN: 978-1-4654-1983-5 (Hardback)

Color reproduction by Alta Image
Printed and bound in China

Discover more at
www.dk.com
www.LEGO.com

Contents

Welcome to Heartlake City

This is Mia. Do you like animals? Mia does! This is her dog, Charlie.

Charlie sleeps in a cool doghouse that Mia helped decorate.

Mia's friends Olivia, Emma, Stephanie, and Andrea love animals, too. The girls enjoy spending time with all their pets. Let's meet some of them.

Jazz

Jazz is Andrea's rabbit. Andrea grows carrots for her furry friend in her garden.

Carrot

Broom

Jazz makes a big mess
eating his carrots! Andrea
gets to work tidying the hutch
with a broom.

Water

Bucket

Scarlett

Scarlett is Olivia's puppy.
Olivia and Mia train her
to perform in dog shows.
She is great at balancing.

Seesaw

Ball skills

Scarlett wants to improve her soccer skills. She is learning how to weave a soccer ball in between cones. What a great trick!

Doghouse

Bone

Cotton

Stephanie is looking after a newborn lamb named Cotton.

Cotton has gotten very dirty playing outside. Stephanie gently washes her woolly fleece.

Snow
There is another new arrival at Heartlake Stables. Olivia helped deliver a beautiful white foal named Snow.

Brush

Tub

Felix and Max

Felix the cat likes to pounce and play on the climbing tower the girls have built for him.

Scratching post

Max the puppy thinks it is much more fun to climb up and down the seesaw outside his playhouse.

Slide

Snack

Ruby

Ruby is Stephanie's horse. They are entering a jumping competition together.

Bridle

They have been practicing for months! Now Stephanie is sure that Ruby is ready to compete. Good luck, you two!

Saddle

Lady

Lady the poodle is at
Heartlake Pet Salon.
She loves being washed in
the bath and having her
hair brushed and trimmed.

Emma

Now Lady is ready to show off her new look on a walk in the park.

Accessories
The salon has so many great accessories, such as bows, clips, and crowns. It's hard to pick just one.

Water dish

Daisy

Daisy is Stephanie's bunny. She has learned how to perform amazing magic tricks with Mia.

Magic
wand

Hat

Daisy also helps Stephanie look for lost animals on a cool patrol bike.

Playing cards

Bella

Bella is Mia's horse.
Mia makes sure Bella
is fit and healthy.

Mia once took Bella to the
vet because she had a stone
stuck in her hoof. Ouch!

Sophie

Sophie is the Heartlake City vet. The girls take their pets to her for checkups. Sophie makes sure the pets get the help and care they need.

Mane

Tail

Hay

21

On the Ranch

Mia works on her grandparents' ranch with her friend Liza.

Liza

Horses, rabbits, cats, and hens live on Sunshine Ranch, so it is very busy and noisy. The girls have to work hard to keep the place in order.

Cherry tree
This beautiful tree makes the perfect shady spot for the girls to rest in.

Snow

Felix

Jazz

Busy Workers

There are many jobs to do on the ranch. Liza loves feeding carrots to the rabbits.

Liza

Mia collects eggs that
Clara the hen has laid.
The eggs will make
a delicious lunch!

Coop

Egg

Maxie and Goldie

The girls look after Maxie the cat from their club tree house.

The friends also take care of Goldie the bird. When he broke his wing, they built him a beautiful birdhouse to recover in.

Birdhouse

Tree house

Telescope

Quiz

1. Who does Jazz belong to?

2. What is the name of the newborn lamb?

3. Which pet has a seesaw outside his playhouse?

4. Which pet enters a jumping competition?

5. Where does Lady go to get her hair trimmed?

6. Which pet performs magic tricks with Mia?

7. Which pet once got a stone stuck in her hoof?

8. Who loves feeding carrots to rabbits on Sunshine Ranch?

9. Where do the girls look after Maxie the cat?

10. What did Goldie the bird break?

Answers on
page 31

Glossary

accessories
extra items that can be worn

bridle
straps used to control a horse

checkup
medical exam

compete
try to win something

coop
place where chickens live

doghouse
shelter for a dog

fleece
soft, warm covering of a sheep

foal
baby horse

ranch
large farm where lots of animals live together

recover
get better

vet
doctor for animals

weave
move in and out

Index

Answers to the quiz on pages 28 and 29:
1. Andrea 2. Cotton 3. Max the puppy
4. Ruby 5. To Heartlake Pet Salon 6. Daisy
7. Bella 8. Liza 9. From their club tree house
10. His wing

Here are some other DK Readers you might enjoy.

Level 2

LEGO® Friends: Let's Go Riding
Join the friends at Heartlake Stables and the Riding School—and meet their favorite horses.

The Little Ballerina
It's the day of the big performance at Laura's ballet school when disaster strikes. Discover how Laura helps save the day.

The Great Panda Tale
Join the excitement as a zoo gets ready to welcome a new panda baby.

Level 3

LEGO® Friends: Friends Forever
Come meet Olivia and her fabulous new best friends Emma, Andrea, Stephanie, and Mia.

LEGO® Friends: Summer Adventures
Enjoy a summer of fun in Heartlake City with Emma, Mia, Andrea, Stephanie, Olivia, and friends.

Rainforest Explorer
Through her blog, Zoe shares the thrills as she travels through the Amazon rainforest.